Sports Day

JANE LAWES

ILLUSTRATED BY SARAH JENNINGS

BLOOMSBURY EDUCATION
Bloomsbury Publishing Plc
50 Bedford Square, London, WC1B 3DP, UK

BLOOMSBURY, BLOOMSBURY EDUCATION and the Diana logo are
trademarks of Bloomsbury Publishing Plc

First published in Great Britain in 2018 by Bloomsbury Publishing Plc

A catalogue record for this book is available from the British Library

ISBN: PB: 978-1-4729-5559-3; ePDF: 978-1-4729-5560-9; ePub: 978-1-4729-5558-6

2 4 6 8 10 9 7 5 3 1

Printed and bound in China by Leo Paper Products, Heshan, Guangdong

To find out more about our authors and books visit www.bloomsbury.com
and sign up for our newsletters

Chapter One

Green Class were sitting on the floor in their classroom. Miss Newton waited for them to be quiet.

"Tomorrow is a special day," she said. "It's going to be Sports Day!"

Most of the children cheered but Emmie felt her heart sink.

"I'm rubbish at sports," she whispered to her best friend, Shivani. Shivani looked very excited about Sports Day. She was the best in their class at running. "There must be one race you're good at," said Shivani.

"I don't think so," Emmie said, sadly.
"You must each choose one race to take
part in," said Miss Newton.
Shivani shot her hand into the air.
"Yes, Shivani?" asked Miss Newton.
"What will the different races be?"
Shivani asked.

"There will be a running race, an egg-and-spoon race, a three-legged race and a sack race. There will also be long-jump, to see who can jump the furthest," said Miss Newton. Everybody started talking at once about which race they wanted to do.

But Emmie didn't know how to choose.
"I'm no good at any of them," she said.
"I can't choose!"
"Let's practise at break time," said
Shivani. "You can find out which
one you're good at. That will help
you decide!"

Chapter Two

When their morning lessons were over, Emmie and her friends dashed out into the playground.

"Let's have a running race," said Shivani.

"Good idea!" said Emmie. "It might help to practise before Sports Day."

Joe and Oskar put their school jumpers on the ground to mark the start line. "The fence is the finish line," said Joe, pointing to the end of the playground. They all stood in a row at the start line.

"Ready, set, GO!" shouted Oskar. They were off!

Emmie ran as fast as she could.
She heard her shoes slapping on the
playground, quick, quick, quick. Her
long blonde hair flew out behind her as
she raced, and the cool breeze rushed
past her cheeks. It felt wonderful!

But then she saw Shivani pass her, reaching for the finish line. Joe and Oskar ran past her, too. Shivani got to the fence and turned around with a big smile. She was the winner! Joe and Oskar finished next.

Emmie came last. She didn't want to be last on Sports Day, running all by herself when the others had already finished.

"I can't do that race tomorrow," she said, trying to catch her breath. "Never mind," said Shivani. "Maybe you'll be the best at something else."

"Are you going to choose the
running race?" Emmie asked. "You'll
probably win!"
"I don't know," said Shivani. "Let's try
all the other races too!"
"What's next?" asked Joe.
"How about long-jump?" said Oskar.
"Let's see who can jump the furthest!"

"Yes!" Emmie said brightly. She was no good at running, but jumping was totally different. Maybe this would be the answer to her Sports Day problem.

Chapter Three

Emmie found a long twig and placed it on the ground to mark the line they would all jump from. Shivani, Oskar and Joe collected some big stones to use as markers to show how far they could each jump.

"I'll go first!" said Oskar. He walked
back behind the twig. He took a big run
up and when he reached the start line
he leaped into the air. He landed with a
thud and almost toppled over. Shivani
rushed in with a stone and placed it
beside his feet.

"My turn!" said Shivani.
Emmie stood to the side holding a stone to mark how far Shivani jumped. She watched her best friend fly through the air and then she rushed to put the stone down where Shivani landed.

She hadn't jumped as far as Oskar, but she wasn't too far behind. Emmie looked back towards the twig, feeling worried. She didn't think she would be able to leap as far as the others could.

Joe went next. He took a huge run up and when he jumped, he kicked his legs through the air as if he was running. He beat Shivani, but didn't go as far as Oskar.

Emmie stood behind the twig, ready for her turn.

"Go on, Emmie!" cheered Shivani.

Emmie took a deep breath. She sprinted forwards, hurtling towards the twig. When she reached it, she leaped into the air. She felt like she was flying! Her face lit up with a grin. She landed, and didn't fall over.

But when she looked back to see how far she had jumped, her heart sank again. She was way behind the others! She had come last again.

The bell rang for the end of break, and they all trooped back to the classroom.

"I can't do long-jump tomorrow," said Emmie.

"Don't worry," said Shivani. "There are still other races we can try."
But Emmie was worried. She was running out of time to choose an event, and so far she hadn't been good at any of them.

Chapter Four

Emmie's class had P.E. after break. "We're going to practise the egg-and-spoon race," said Miss Newton. She had a bag full of big spoons from the kitchen and some tennis balls, which she handed out to everyone.

"Start by balancing the ball on the spoon," Miss Newton told them. "And then try walking or running with it." Emmie held her spoon out in front of her and placed the bright orange ball on it. She was no good at running or jumping but maybe this was the race for her.

She took a few steps forward and the ball rolled off and bounced away across the grass. Emmie chased after it and put it back on the spoon. This time, when she started walking, she tried to keep the spoon straight so that the ball didn't fall off.

She was being so careful that she didn't see Shivani coming towards her. Crash! They walked right into each other, and their tennis balls bounced away. They both laughed and ran to get them back.

It was hard to walk and keep the ball on the spoon at the same time. Emmie and Shivani spent more time chasing after escaping balls than they did holding them!

"Let's have a race!" called Miss Newton. Everyone stood in a line. "The finish is the football goal-posts," she said. "Ready, set, GO!"
The whole class rushed forwards at once. Emmie's ball fell off her spoon as soon as she started running.

She bent to pick it up, and saw that Shivani had the same problem. They both laughed, then began to run again. Emmie tried her hardest, but the ball wanted to go everywhere but on her spoon! She could see that Joe had almost won the race.

But Shivani wasn't any good at this one, either. They came joint last, but Emmie didn't mind. She had laughed so much during the race that her tummy hurt and she couldn't stop smiling. "Maybe I shouldn't choose the egg-and-spoon race for Sports Day," said Emmie.

"Maybe not," Shivani agreed. She tried to balance the ball on her spoon again and it fell off straight away. They both giggled. "This is not the best race for me," said Shivani.

Emmie felt worried again. The problem was, it didn't seem like *any* of the races were the best race for her.

Chapter Five

At the end of the day, Miss Newton asked the class which races they would like to do for Sports Day. Emmie still couldn't choose. Everybody else knew exactly what they were good at, but Emmie felt like she wasn't good at anything at all.

She felt as if she might cry.

"Long-jump!" said Oskar, when Miss Newton asked him which one he wanted to take part in.

"Egg-and-spoon race, please," said Joe.

"What about you, Emmie?" asked Miss Newton.

"I don't know," Emmie said in a tiny voice. "I'm not good at any of them."

"Pick the one you think will be the most fun," said Miss Newton.

Emmie hadn't thought of it like that! She had been trying to find out which race she would be the best at – she had forgotten that Sports Day was meant to be fun, too.

"Which one are you going to do?" Miss Newton asked. But now Emmie had a different problem. She remembered the feeling of running through the wind as she raced her friends, and flying through the air in the long-jump, and laughing until her tummy hurt in the egg-and-spoon race.

"I still can't choose," she said, with a big smile. "I enjoyed all of them!"
"Let's do the three-legged race together," said Shivani. "The other races are fun, but running as a team will be the best of all."

"I thought you wanted to win the running race," said Emmie.

"I've changed my mind," said Shivani. "I might be best at running, but it would be much more fun to do the three-legged race with you."

Emmie grinned at her best friend.
Sports Day was going to be great!

Chapter Six

The next morning, Emmie and Shivani used a ribbon to tie their ankles together. They walked all over the playground with their arms around each other's waists and their feet tied together, practising for the three-legged race.

When it was time for Sports Day to start, they changed into their P.E. kit and went out to the school field. Lots of parents had come to watch. Emmie waved to Mum and Dad and they smiled back.

Joe won the egg-and-spoon race, and Emmie clapped and cheered for him. Oskar came first in the long-jump competition and Emmie gave him a high-five. Then it was time for the three-legged race.

Miss Newton tied Emmie and Shivani's ankles together. There were three other pairs from their class in the race. "Ready, set, GO!" shouted Miss Newton.

Emmie and Shivani lurched forwards, counting together so that they ran in time with each other and didn't fall over. They raced past Amy and Rachel, and they shot past Tom and Sachin. Felix and Lola were winning, but Emmie and Shivani were catching up.

"We can do it!" Emmie said to Shivani. She felt her feet hitting the ground in time with Shivani's and her hair flying out behind her. Running and laughing with Shivani felt even better than running by herself.

They crossed the finish line, two steps
behind Felix and Lola.

"That was great!" said Emmie.

"We almost won," said Shivani.

"It was so much fun, it feels like we
did win," said Emmie.

"We were a good team," said Shivani.
"Let's do the three-legged race together
every year," said Emmie.

They went back to sit with the rest of their class, walking with their feet still tied together and their arms linked.

47

Emmie couldn't wait for next year's
Sports Day!